DADDY FARTYPANTS

EMER STAMP • MATT HUNT

For Dick Stamp, the original
Daddy Fartypants – E.S.

For my family – M.H.

ORCHARD BOOKS

First published in Great Britain in 2019 by
The Watts Publishing Group

1 3 5 7 9 10 8 6 4 2

Text © Emer Stamp 2019
Illustrations © Matt Hunt 2019

A CIP catalogue record for this book is
available from the British Library.

HB ISBN 978 1 40835 633 3
PB ISBN 978 1 40835 635 7

MIX
Paper from
responsible sources
FSC
www.fsc.org
FSC® C104740

Printed and bound in China

Orchard Books
An imprint of Hachette Children's Group
Part of The Watts Publishing Group Limited
Carmelite House, 50 Victoria Embankment
London EC4Y 0DZ

An Hachette UK Company
www.hachette.co.uk

www.hachettechildrens.co.uk

DADDY FARTYPANTS

EMER STAMP • MATT HUNT

ORCHARD

Daddy Fartypants was a very windy bear.

It didn't matter where he was . . .

. . . or what he was doing . . .

his bottom blasts were **epic**.
And to make matters worse . . .

Daddy Fartypants always, always,
ALWAYS blamed someone else.

"It was the baby!"

FLUURRRRP!

"waahh!"

TRRRUUUMMP!

"The busker!"

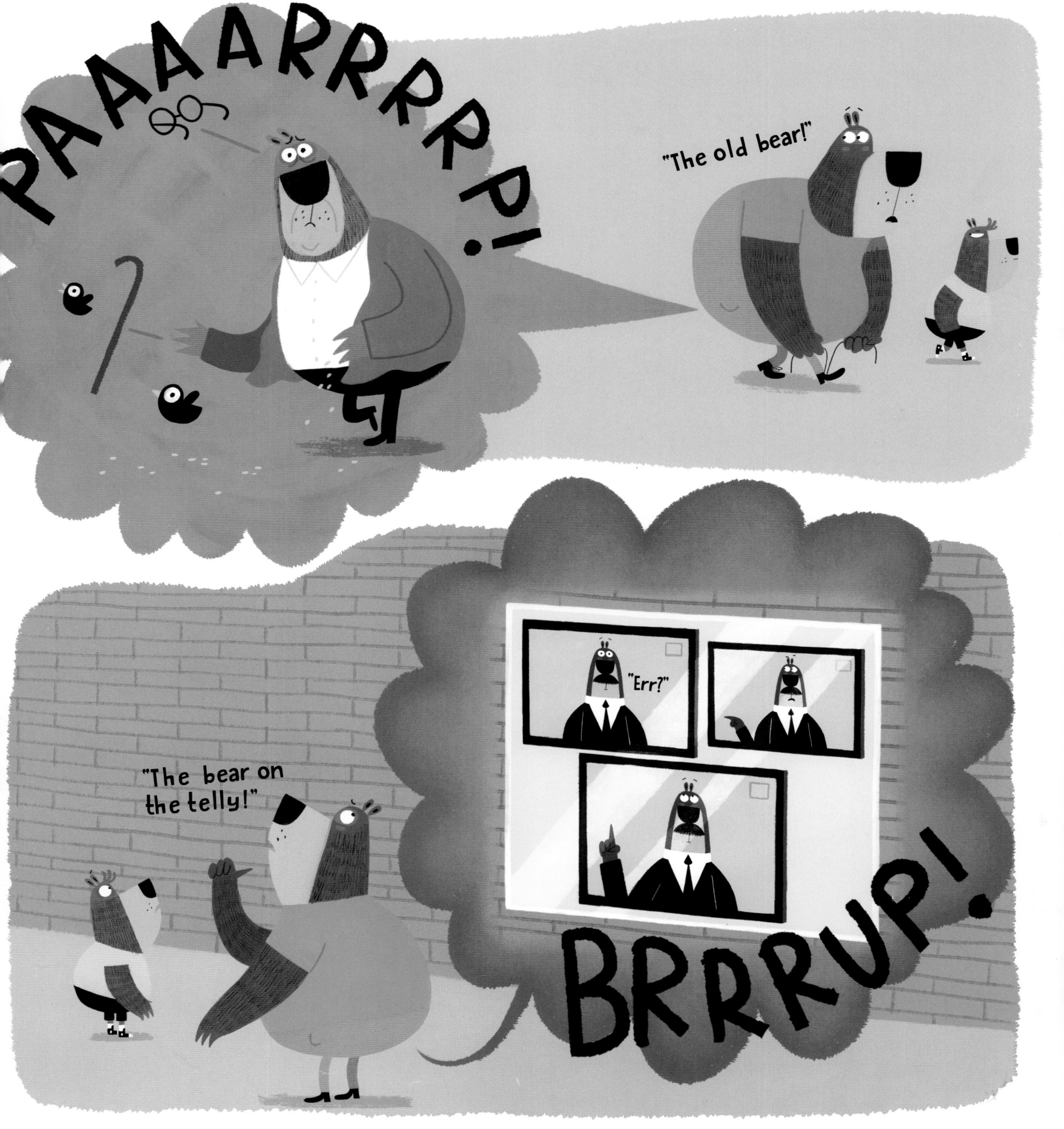
PAAAARRRRP!
"The old bear!"
"Err?"
"The bear on the telly!"
BRRRUP!

Even when it was REALLY obvious, Daddy Fartypants never said "sorry" or "pardon", or "excuse me, please".

"It was the snail."

No, Daddy Fartypants never,
ever, ever, ever, EVER . . .

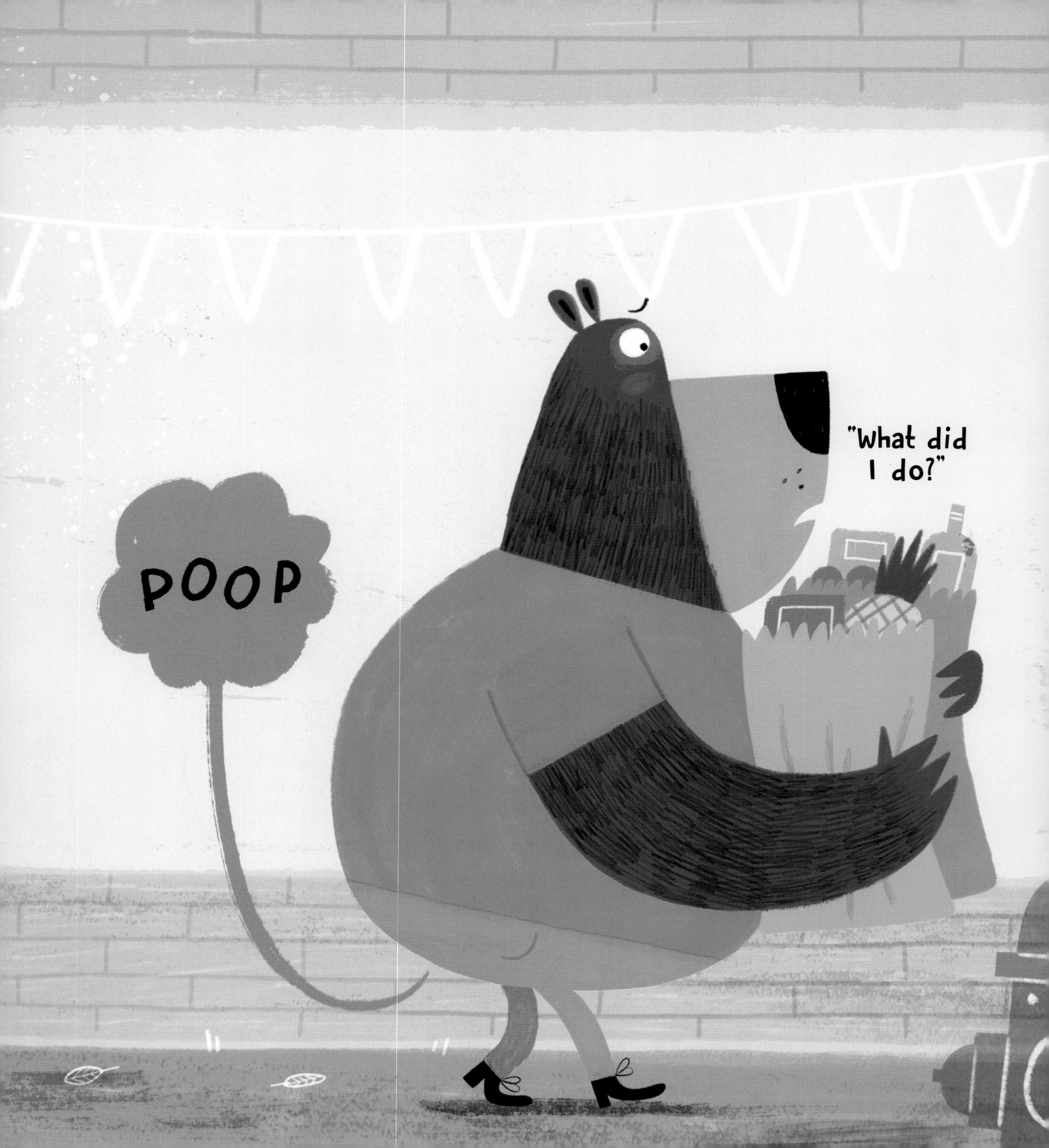
POOP
"What did I do?"

Then, one day after school, Daddy Fartypants met the lovely new teacher, Miss Lovelybear.

"How lovely to meet you."

But as he went to shake her hand . . .

Miss Lovelybear let out a rip-roaring . . .

"Yuck!"

"Disgusting!"

"Pooey!"

"What DID you have for lunch?"

BWWWWAAAR

RRPPFFFFP!

"That pongs!"

"Oh my!"

"Gr-ross!"

"Squelchy!"

Everyone heard it.

But Miss Lovelybear didn't say "sorry"
or "pardon" or "excuse me, please". Instead she said . . .

Daddy Fartypants was shocked.

"W . . . what?"

He was outraged.

"How dare you!"

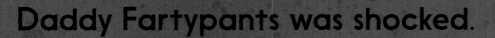

He was upset.

"Everyone thinks it was ME!"

But, most of all, he was ashamed.

And that night he made a promise . . .

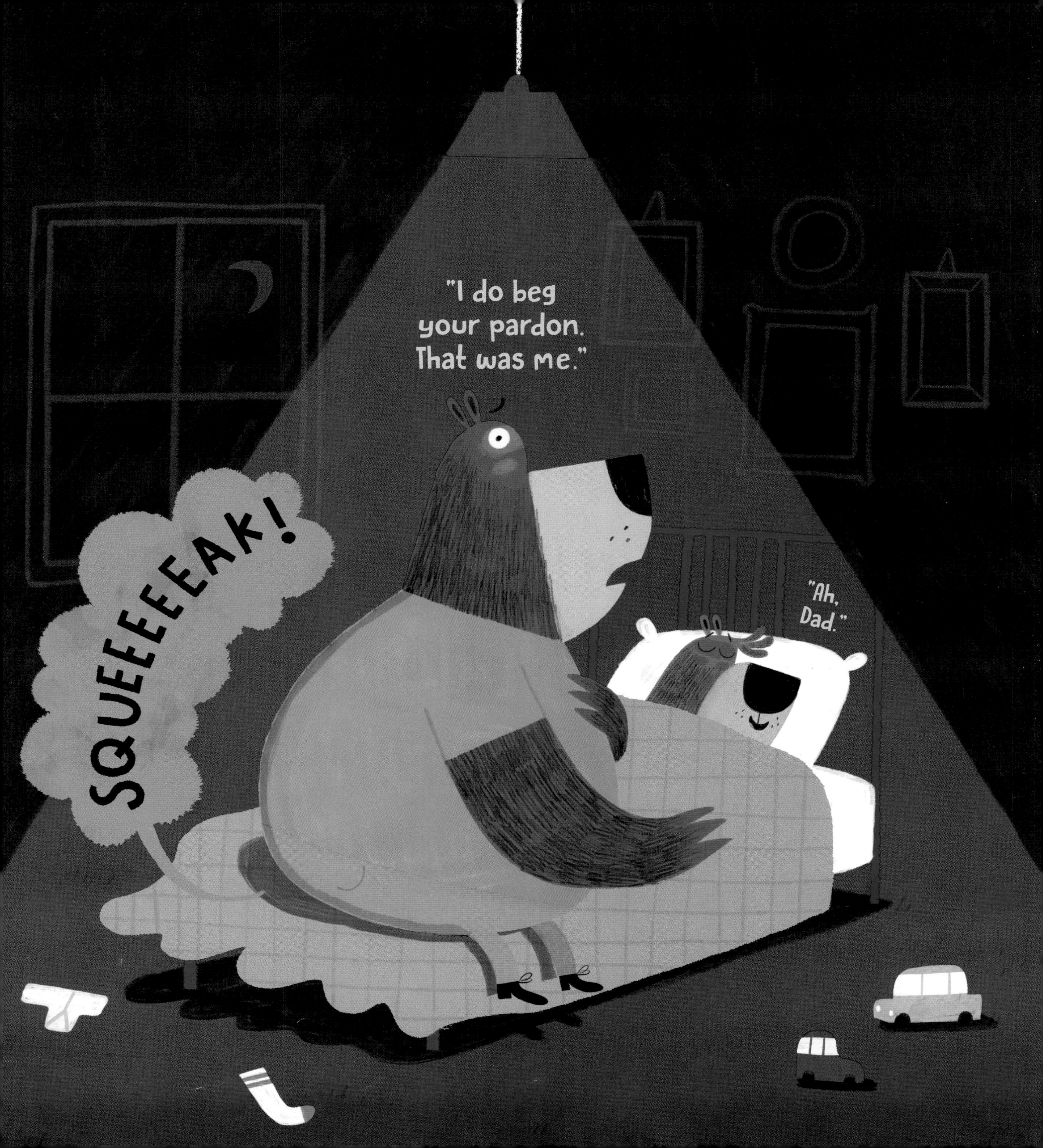
"I do beg
your pardon.
That was me."
SQUEEEEEAK!
"Ah,
Dad."

Daddy Fartypants is STILL a very windy bear. But no matter where he is . . .

. . . or what he's doing . . .

PUFF

. . . he always, always, always, **always** . . .

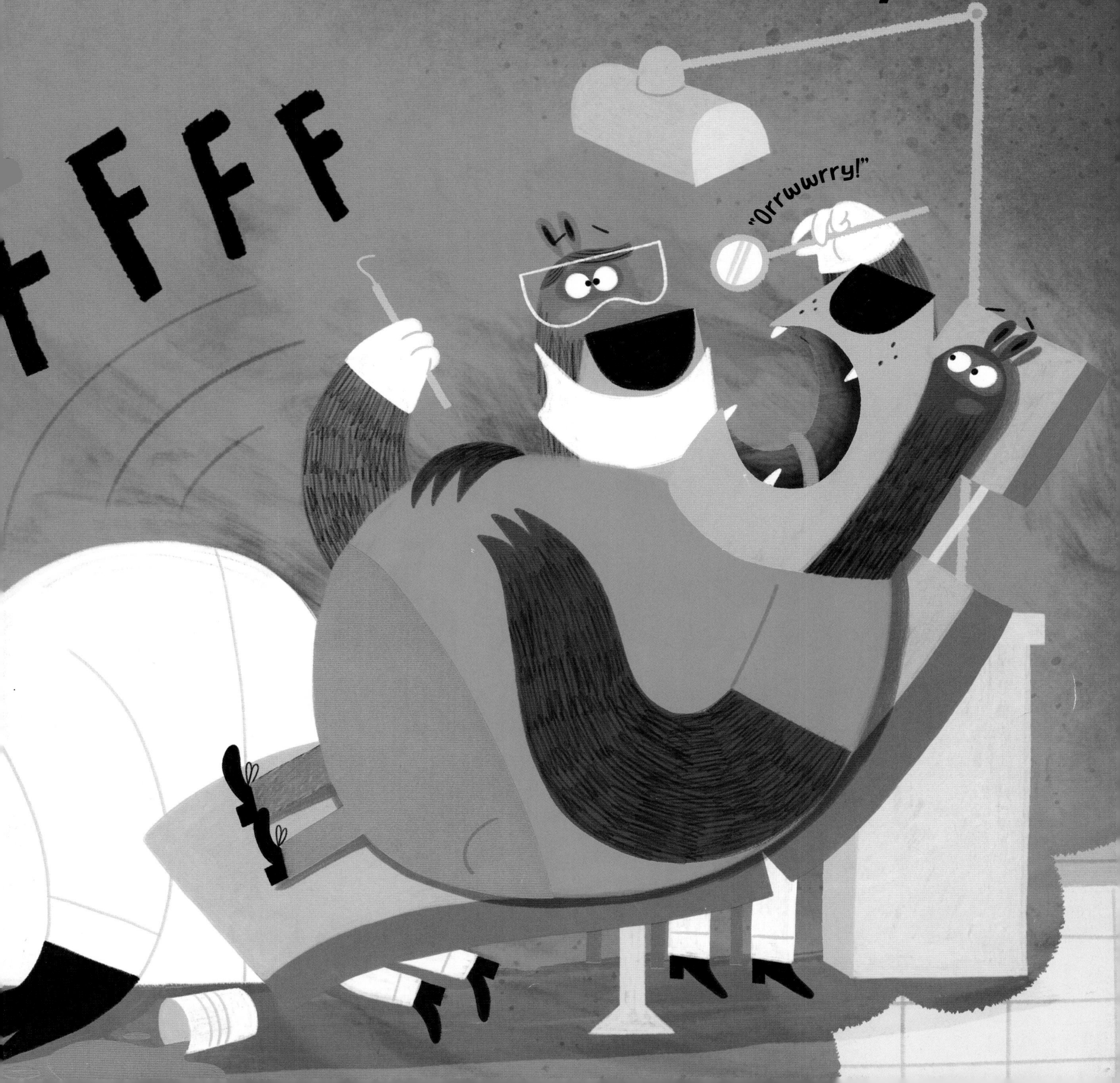

PPPRRRRRRRRRRRRRRRRRUPT.

. . . owns up.

"Oops, sorry!"

"I love you, Dad."

POP!